10 Minute Tales

D0525804

How Poohsticks Began

When you see these symbols:

Read aloud
Read aloud to your child.

Read alone
Support your child as they read alone.

Read along
Read along with your child.

FSC
www.fsc.org
MIX
Paper from responsible sources
FSC® C018306

Egmont is passionate about helping to preserve the world's remaining ancient forests. We only use paper from legal and sustainable forest sources.

This book is made from paper certified by the Forestry Stewardship Council® (FSC®), an organisation dedicated to promoting responsible management of forest resources. For more information on the FSC®, please visit www.fsc.org. To learn more about Egmont's sustainable paper policy, please visit www.egmont.co.uk/ethical

EGMONT

This story takes place at Poohsticks Bridge.

Can you see it on the map?

One day, Pooh was walking through the forest humming to himself, when he came across some fir cones lying on the ground. He picked one up to take home.

He had just reached a bridge, and not looking where he was going, he tripped and the fir cone fell into the river.

"Bother," said Pooh, as he lay down to watch the river. Suddenly, there was his fir cone. "That's funny," said Pooh. "I dropped it on the other side and it came out on this side! I wonder if it would do it again?" And he went back for some more fir cones.

Read alone

Pooh dropped a fir cone into the river and it floated under the bridge.

Read aloud   Read along

The fir cones all came out as Pooh thought they would. Then he dropped one big one and one little one, and the big one came out first, and the little one came out last, and they were both Pooh's fir cones so he had won twice.

And that was the beginning of the game called Poohsticks, that Pooh and his friends used to play with sticks instead of fir cones, because it was easier to tell the difference between sticks.

Read alone

Pooh dropped more fir cones into the river.
He watched to see which floated to the other
side first. And so the game of Poohsticks began.

Read aloud   Read along

One day Pooh, Piglet, Rabbit and Roo were playing Poohsticks. They had dropped their sticks in and then hurried to the other side of the bridge to see whose stick would come out first.

"I can see mine!" cried Roo. "No, I can't, it's something else. Can you see yours, Pooh?"

"No," said Pooh.

"I expect my stick's stuck," said Roo.

Read alone

One day, Pooh, Piglet, Rabbit and Roo
were playing Poohsticks on the bridge.

"I can see yours, Piglet," said Pooh suddenly. "It's coming over to my side."

Piglet got very excited because that meant he was winning. "Are you sure it's mine?" he squeaked.

"Yes, because it's grey. Here it comes! A very – big – grey – oh, no, it isn't, it's Eeyore."

And out floated Eeyore.

Read alone

Pooh thought he could see Piglet's stick, but it was Eeyore! He was floating in the river!

"Eeyore, what are you doing there?" said Rabbit.
"I'm waiting for someone to help me out of the river,"
said Eeyore.

"But, Eeyore," said Pooh, "what can we – I mean, how shall
we – do you think if we –"
"Yes," said Eeyore. "One of those would be just the thing.
Thank you, Pooh."

Read alone

Eeyore was waiting for someone to rescue him, but Pooh didn't know what to do.

Read aloud

Read along

"I've got a sort of idea," said Pooh at last, "but I don't suppose it's a very good one."

"Go on, Pooh," said Rabbit.

"Well, if we threw stones into the river on one side of Eeyore, the stones would make waves, and the waves would wash him to the other side."

"Good idea," said Rabbit.

Pooh found a big stone.

Read alone

Then Pooh had an idea. He got a big stone to throw into the river near Eeyore, to make a big wave.

Pooh leant over the bridge with his stone.

"I'm not throwing it, I'm dropping it, Eeyore," Pooh explained. "And then I can't miss — I mean I can't hit you." Pooh dropped his stone. There was a loud splash, and Eeyore disappeared.

Read alone

Pooh dropped the stone into the river and Eeyore disappeared.

Read aloud   Read along

It was an anxious moment. Then something grey showed for a moment by the river bank. It slowly got bigger and bigger and at last Eeyore came out. With a shout they rushed towards him.

"Well done, Pooh," said Rabbit kindly. Eeyore was very wet indeed.

Read alone

At last Eeyore slowly climbed out of the river.
He was very wet.

Read aloud   **Read along**

"How did you fall in, in the first place, Eeyore?"
asked Rabbit.
"Somebody BOUNCED me. I was just thinking
by the side of the river, when I received a loud BOUNCE,"
said Eeyore.
"But who did it?" asked Roo.
"I expect it was Tigger," said Piglet nervously.

There was a loud noise behind them, and through the
hedge came Tigger himself.

Read alone

Eeyore was cross. He said he had been bounced into the river by Tigger.

Read aloud   **Read along**

"Hallo, everybody," said Tigger cheerfully. Rabbit becam
very important suddenly.

"Tigger," he said. "What happened just now?"

"Just when?" said Tigger.

"When you bounced Eeyore into the river."

"I didn't bounce him. I had a cough, and said, GRRR-OPPPHH!"

"That's what I call bouncing," said Eeyore.

"I didn't bounce, I coughed," said Tigger crossly.

"Bouncy or coffy, it's all the same at the bottom of the river,"
said Eeyore.

Read alone

Tigger said he didn't bounce. He coughed loudly, and that's why Eeyore fell into the river.

Read aloud   Read along

Christopher Robin came down to the bridge and saw all the animals there.

"It's like this, Christopher Robin," began Rabbit. "Tigger—"

"All I did was I coughed," said Tigger.

"He bounced," said Eeyore.

"Well, I sort of boffed," said Tigger.

"Hush!" said Rabbit. "What does Christopher Robin think about it all? That's the point."

"Well," said Christopher Robin, not quite sure what it was all about. "I think we all ought to play Poohsticks."

When Christopher Robin came to the bridge he listened to Tigger and Eeyore. He said they should all just play Poohsticks now.

So they did.
And Eeyore, who
had never played it
before, won more times
than anybody else; and Roo fell in
twice, the first time by accident and the second time on
purpose, because he saw Kanga coming and knew he'd have
to go to bed anyhow.

So then Rabbit said he'd go home with Kanga and Roo;
and Tigger and Eeyore went off together. Christopher
Robin and Pooh and Piglet were left on the bridge by
themselves.

Read alone

The friends played for a long time.
Then it was bedtime for Kanga, Roo,
Rabbit, Tigger and Eeyore.

Read aloud   Read along

For a long time they looked at the river beneath them, saying nothing, for it felt very quiet and peaceful on this summer afternoon.

"Tigger is all right, really," said Piglet lazily.
"Of course he is," said Christopher Robin.
"Everybody is really," said Pooh. "That's what I think, but I don't suppose I'm right."
"Of course you are," said Christopher Robin.

Read alone

Christopher Robin, Pooh and Piglet sat
watching the river. It had been a lovely day.

Can you see Pooh? How about Rabbit and Roo?

Where's Eeyore? What about Piglet?

Enjoy more titles
from the Winnie-the-Pooh range . . .

Winnie-the-Pooh
and the
Grand Christmas Surprise

Illustrations by Andrew Grey

With five special letters and press-out Christmas decorations!

Winnie-the-Pooh
and the
Trouble
with
Bees

Illustrations by Andrew Grey

Winnie-the-Pooh
A Perfect Day for
Poohsticks

A
Peek-through
Book

Winnie-the-Pooh
(and friends!)
Hide and Peek

Find the
4 forest
friends

Winnie-the-Pooh
Touch and Feel

Illustrations by Andrew Grey

Winnie
-the-
Pooh

Buggy
Book

Winnie-the-Pooh
Pooh's Snowy Day

Tigger

Buggy
Book